Let's Enjoy Masterpie

Bible Stories
聖經故事

Adaptor   Brian J. Stuart
Illustrator Ludmila Pipchenko

WORDS
350

MP3

Let's Enjoy Masterpieces!

All the beautiful fairy tales and masterpieces that you have encountered during your childhood remain as warm memories in your adulthood. This time, let's indulge in the world of masterpieces through English. You can enjoy the depth and beauty of original works, which you can't enjoy through Chinese translations.

The stories are easy for you to understand because of your familiarity with them. When you enjoy reading, your ability to understand English will also rapidly improve.

This series of *Let's Enjoy Masterpieces* are a special reading comprehension booster program, devised to improve reading comprehension for beginners whose command of English is not satisfactory, or who are elementary, middle, and high school students. With this program, you can enjoy reading masterpieces in English with fun and efficiency.

This carefully planned program is composed of 5 levels, from the beginner level of 350 words to the intermediate and advanced levels of 1,000 words. With this program's level-by-level system, you are able to read famous texts in English and to savor the true pleasure of the world's language.

The program is well conceived, composed of reader-friendly explanations of English expressions and grammar, quizzes to help the student learn vocabulary and understand the meaning of the texts, and fabulous illustrations that adorn every page. In addition, with our "Guide to Listening," not only is reading comprehension enhanced but also listening comprehension skills are highlighted.

In the audio recording of the book, texts are vividly read by professional American voice actors. The texts are rewritten, according to the levels of the readers by an expert editorial staff of native speakers, on the basis of standard American English with the ministry of education recommended vocabulary. Therefore, it will be of great help even for all the students that want to learn English.

Please indulge yourself in the fun of reading and listening to English through *Let's Enjoy Masterpieces*.

Introduction
簡介

The Origin and Meaning of *the Holy Bible*

The Holy Bible was originally referred to as the 'Biblion' in Greek. The word 'Biblion' translates directly into 'book,' but in the 12th century it became known as *the Holy Bible*.

The Holy Bible is divided into two books: *The Old Testament* and *The New Testament*. *The Old Testament* is God's contract and covenant with the Israelites through the peacemaking of Moses. *The New Testament* is the teachings of Christianity through the words of Jesus.

The Old and New Testament are composed of sixty-six books that are a compilation of writings from more than 40 different writers over a 1500-year period. The contents of these books are on a vast scale and record the history of different periods and the religious teachings of Christianity.

The Old Testament starts with the creation and then tells the story of mankind through Adam and Eve, Abraham's family, Moses, and the Jewish exodus from Egypt. Stories about the kings of Israel and the prophets Elijah and Daniel are also included.

Adam   was the first human created by God. Adam was made in the image of God and placed on earth. In ancient Hebrew the name Adam means "earth."

Eve   was the first woman and was created from the rib of Adam. Eve's eating of the forbidden fruit was the first or original sin. As a consequence, God required men to work and take care of the family, and women were given the difficult and painful task of childbearing.

Moses   was the leader who brought the Israelites out of slavery in Egypt and led them to the Promised Land.

David   was a young shepherd who became famous for a using a sling and stone to slay the giant Goliath. Later, he became the second king of Israel and created a grand government.

Solomon   was the son of David and became the third king of Israel. Solomon was famous as a really wise king who used his wisdom to determine who was the mother of a baby. Solomon's successful reign of forty years speaks well for his intelligence, ability, and statesmanship.

Daniel   was a Hebrew prophet. His name means, "My judge is God." He fought against harassment and conspiracies from other religions. Daniel maintained the law of God and gained respect by impressing the pagan king, Darius.

HOW TO USE THIS BOOK
本書使用說明

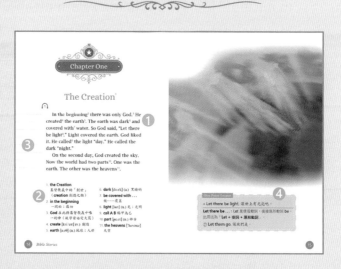

① Original English texts

It is easy to understand the meaning of the text, because the text is divided phrase by phrase and sentence by sentence.

② Explanation of the vocabulary

The words and expressions that include vocabulary above the elementary level are clearly defined.

③ Response notes

Spaces are included in the book so you can take notes about what you don't understand or what you want to remember.

④ One point lesson

In-depth analyses of major grammar points and expressions help you to understand sentences with difficult grammar.

∩ *Audio Recording*

In the audio recording, native speakers narrate the texts in standard American English. By combining the written words and the audio recording, you can listen to English with great ease.

Audio books have been popular in Britain and America for many decades. They allow the listener to experience the proper word pronunciation and sentence intonation that add important meaning and drama to spoken English. Students will benefit from listening to the recording twenty or more times.

After you are familiar with the text and recording, listen once more with your eyes closed to check your listening comprehension. Finally, after you can listen with your eyes closed and understand every word and every sentence, you are then ready to mimic the native speaker.

Then you should make a recording by reading the text yourself. Then play both recordings to compare your oral skills with those of a native speaker.

HOW TO IMPROVE READING ABILITY

如何增進英文閱讀能力

① *Catch key words*

Read the key words in the sentences and practice catching the gist of the meaning of the sentence. You might question how working with a few important words could enhance your reading ability. However, it's quite effective. If you continue to use this method, you will find out that the key words and your knowledge of people and situations enables you to understand the sentence.

② *Divide long sentences*

Read in chunks of meaning, dividing sentences into meaningful chunks of information. In the book, chunks are arranged in sentences according to meaning. If you consider the sentences backwards or grammatically, your reading speed will be slow and you will find it difficult to listen to English.

You are ready to move to a more sophisticated level of comprehension when you find that narrowly focusing on chunks is irritating. Instead of considering the chunks, you will make it a habit to read the sentence from the beginning to the end to figure out the meaning of the whole.

③ Make inferences and assumptions

Making inferences and assumptions are part of your ability. If you don't know, try to guess the meaning of the words. Although you don't know all the words in context, don't go straight to the dictionary. Developing an ability to make inferences in the context is important.

The first way to figure out the meaning of a word is from its context. If you cannot make head or tail out of the meaning of a word, look at what comes before or after it. Ask yourself what can happen in such a situation. Make your best guess as to the word's meaning. Then check the explanations of the word in the book or look up the word in a dictionary.

④ Read a lot and reread the same book many times

There is no shortcut to mastering English. Only if you do a lot of reading will you make your way to the summit. Read fun and easy books with an average of less than one new word per page. Try to immerse yourself in English as often as you can.

Spend time "swimming" in English. Language learning research has shown that immersing yourself in English will help you improve your English, even though you may not be aware of what you're learning.

CONTENTS

Introduction 4

How to Use This Book 6

How to Improve Reading Ability 8

Before You Read 12

Chapter One

   The Creation 14

   Adam and Eve 20

      Comprehension Quiz 26

Chapter Two

   Cain and Abel 28

   Noah's Ark 34

   Tower of Babel 38

      Comprehension Quiz 42

Before You Read 44

Chapter Three

   Moses and the Burning Bush 46

   Escape from Egypt 50

The Ten Commandments 54

   Comprehension Quiz 60

Before You Read 62

Chapter Four

   Samson 64

   David and Goliath 70

      Comprehension Quiz 76

Chapter Five

   King Solomon 78

   Daniel and the Lions 82

      Comprehension Quiz 88

Appendixes

❶ Basic Grammar 92

❷ Guide to Listening Comprehension ... 96

❸ Listening Guide 100

❹ Listening Comprehension 104

Translation 108

Answers 124

The Creation
創世

heaven
天堂

God
Lord
上帝

light
光

Let there be light.
讓世上有光吧。

create 創造
bless 賜福
rule 治理

a flock of birds
一群鳥

Let there be fish in the sea
and birds in the air.
讓海中有魚，空中有鳥吧。

run fast
快跑

A zebra is running fast.
有一匹斑馬正飛快跑著。

rest
休息

A goat is resting behind a rock.
有一隻山羊正在一塊岩石後面休息。

mountain 山

valley 谷

field
原野

earth
大地

fall asleep
睡著

A cat fell asleep in the field.
一隻貓在草地上睡著了。

move around
四處移動

stream
溪流

plant
植物

grain
穀類

herb
草本植物

fruit
水果

A tortoise is moving around.
一隻烏龜正在四處走動。

Before You Read

cloud 雲

day 晝

The Garden of Eden
伊甸園

night 夜

The Apple Tree
蘋果樹

good 善
evil 惡

If you eat those apples,
you will know about good and evil.
如果你吃了這些蘋果，
就能體驗到善與惡。

moon 月亮
star 星星
planet 星球

snake 蛇

jealous 妒忌的
trick 哄騙

Eve 夏娃
wife 妻子

Adam 亞當
rib 肋骨

pick 摘
bite 咬

cow 母牛
calf 小牛

thunder 雷
lightning 閃電
storm 暴風雨
heavy rain 豪雨

God was very angry.
上帝非常生氣。
They disobeyed the God.
他們違抗了上帝

feel cold 感到冷
feel afraid 感到害怕
leave 離開

They left the Garden, never to return.
他們離開了伊甸園，永遠不得返回。

The Creation[1]

    In the beginning[2] there was only God.[3] He created[4] the earth[5]. The earth was dark[6] and covered with[7] water. So God said, "Let there be light[8]." Light covered the earth. God liked it. He called[9] the light "day." He called the dark "night."

    On the second day, God created the sky. Now the world had two parts[10]. One was the earth. The other was the heavens[11].

1. **the Creation**
   基督教義中的「創世」
   (**creation** 創造之物)

2. **in the beginning**
   一開始；最初

3. **God** 在此指基督教義中唯一的神(故字首必定大寫)

4. **create** [kri`eɪt] (v.) 創造

5. **earth** [ɜːrθ] (n.) 地球；人世

6. **dark** [dɑːrk] (a.) 黑暗的

7. **be covered with . . .**
   被……覆蓋

8. **light** [laɪt] (n.) 光；光明

9. **call A B** 稱甲為乙

10. **part** [pɑːrt] (n.) 部分

11. **the heavens** [`hevənz]
    天空

Let there be light. 讓世上有光亮吧。

Let there be . . . : Let 是使役動詞，後接原形動詞 be。
此用法為「**Let + 受詞 + 原形動詞**」。

e.g. **Let them go.** 讓他們走。

15

On the third day, God pushed the water aside[1]. The dry land[2] rose up[3]. God called the land "earth." He called the water "seas." Then God created all the plants[4]. He saw that it was good.

On the fourth day, God said, "Day must be divided from[5] night." So He made the sun and the moon. Then God put stars and planets[6] in the sky.

On the fifth day, God said, "Let there be fish in the sea and birds in the air[7]." God blessed[8] all kinds of fish and birds. "Live well and have many children."

1. **push aside** 推開；推到旁邊
   （**aside** 向或在旁邊地）
2. **land** [lænd] (n.) 土地；大地
3. **rise up** 升起；上升
   (rise-rose-risen)
4. **plant** [plænt] (n.) 植物
5. **divide from** 區分；分隔
6. **planet** [ˋplænɪt] (n.) 星球
7. **in the air** 空中
   （**air** 空氣）
8. **bless** [bles] (v.)
   賜福；祝福

◆ On the **fifth** day, God said, "Let there be fish in the sea and birds in the air."
第五天，神說：「讓海中有魚，空中有鳥吧。」

英文中的「序數字」，除了 the first 和 the second，多半從原字變化而來，如 third 來自 three；fourth 來自 four；fifth 來自 five，但要注意，在序數字之前必定要加定冠詞 the。

e.g. This is **the first** snow of this winter.
這是今年冬天的第一場雪。

On the sixth day, God created all the animals. Some animals ran fast over[1] the grass[2]. And some animals hid[3] in the trees. God looked at the animals he created. He was happy. Then God said, "I will make a man and a woman. They will rule over[4] all the animals on land."

God rested[5] on the seventh day. He blessed this day, and made[6] it His special[7] day. This is why man does not work on this day.

1. **over** [`ouvər] (prep.)
   在……之上（反義詞 under）
2. **grass** [græs] (n.) 草；草地
3. **hide** [haɪd] (v.) 躲藏
   (hide-hid-hidden)
4. **rule over** 統治；管轄
5. **rest** [rest] (v.) 休息；歇憩
6. **make A B** 使甲成為乙
   (make-made-made)
7. **special** [`speʃəl] (a.)
   特別的；特殊的

He blessed this day and **made it his special day**.
祂賜福這一天，並且把這一天訂作祂的特別日。

此用法為「**make** + 受詞 + 補語」，指「使甲變成乙」。

e.g. The people **made** him leader. 人民使他成為領袖。

Adam and Eve

4

When God created man, He called him "Adam." God saw that Adam needed a place to live. So He created a beautiful garden called "Eden."

In the middle of¹ the garden, God put a special apple tree. He said to Adam, "You must not eat from my special tree. If you eat those apples, you will know about good and evil² Also, you will grow³ old and die."

1. **in the middle of . . .**
   在……當中
2. **evil** [`i:vəl] (n.) 惡;邪惡
3. **grow + adj.** : 變成;長成
4. **one day** 有一天
5. **lonely** [`lounli] (a.) 寂寞的
6. **helper** [`helpər] (n.) 幫手
7. **fall asleep** 睡著
   (fall-fell-fallen)
8. **rib** [rɪb] (n.) 肋骨
9. **wake up** 醒來
   (wake-woke-woken)
10. **suffer** [`sʌfər] (v.)
    受苦;歷劫
11. **not . . . anything**
    沒有任何……

One day[4], God saw that Adam was lonely[5]. "I will make a helper[6] for this man." When Adam fell asleep[7], God took one of his ribs[8]. From this rib, he made a woman.

Adam woke up[9] and was surprised to see Eve. He thanked God. For a long time, Adam and Eve lived in Eden. They did not suffer[10] or need anything[11].

In the garden, there lived a snake[1]. It was a jealous[2] animal. It did not like to see Adam and Eve so happy.

One day, the snake said to Eve, "Why don't you[3] eat the apples on that tree?"

"We can't," said Eve. "If we eat this fruit, we will die."

"Listen to[4] me," the snake said. "God made you. Why does He want you to die? If you eat this fruit, you will become as powerful[5] as[6] God."

1. **snake** [sneɪk] (n.) 蛇
2. **jealous** [ˈdʒeləs] (a.) 忌妒的
3. **Why don't you . . .?**
   你（們）為什麼不……?
4. **listen to** 用心聽
5. **powerful** [ˈpaʊrfəl] (a.)
   強而有力的
6. **as . . . as . . .** 如……一般

7. **believe** [bɪˈliːv] (v.) 相信
8. **pick** [pɪk] (v.) 摘取；採擷
9. **bite** [baɪt] (v.) 咬
   (bite-bit-bitten)
10. **suddenly** [ˈsʌdənli] (adv.)
    突然地
11. **feel + adj.**：感到或覺得
    (feel-felt-felt)

Eve believed[7] the snake. She picked[8] an apple and bit[9] it. Then she took the apple to Adam. Adam also ate the apple. Suddenly[10], Adam and Eve felt[11] cold and afraid.

One Point Lesson

● It did not like to **see** Adam and Eve **so happy**.
牠不高興看到亞當和夏娃這麼快樂。

see + 受詞 + 形容詞補語：這個句型表示看見（或看出）某某如何如何。

e.g. I saw my father angry. 我看見（看出）家父生氣了。

🎧 6

When God saw Adam and Eve, He knew that they ate the apple from the tree. "What did you do?"

Eve said, "The snake tricked[1] me. He told me I should[2] eat the fruit."

Now God was very angry. "Leave[3] here," he said to them. "You have disobeyed[4] me. Now you must work hard for[5] your food. You will know pain[6] and sorrow[7]. You will also grow old and die."

Adam and Eve left the Garden of Eden, never to return[8].

1. **trick** [trɪk] (v.) 用計誘騙
2. **should** 可以；無妨
3. **leave** [li:v] (v.) 離開；離去
   (leave-left-left)
4. **disobey** [ˌdɪsə`beɪ] (v.)
   違逆；違背
   （反義字：obey 服從）
5. **work for** . . . 為……工作；
   工作以換取……
6. **pain** [peɪn] (n.) 痛苦；疼痛
7. **sorrow** [`sɑ:rou] (n.)
   悲傷；憂傷
8. **return** [rɪ`tɜ:rn] (v.) 返回

One Point Lesson

• **When God saw** them, He knew that they ate the apple from the tree.
神見到亞當和夏娃時，就知道他們吃了那株樹上的蘋果。

「**When** + 主詞 + 動詞，主詞 + 動詞」：
從屬子句與主要句子的時態相同，表示兩件事同時發生。

e.g. **When I woke up**, it began to rain.
當我醒過來後，就開始下雨了。

A Crosswords.

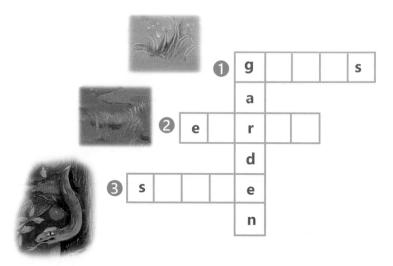

① g _ _ _ s
  a
② e _ r _ _
  d
③ s _ _ _ e
  n

B Write down the right ordinal number.

God created the dry land on the _third_ day.

① God created all the animals on the _____ day.

② God created man on the _____ day.

③ God created light on the _____ day.

④ God created the sun and the moon on the _____ day.

⑤ God rested on the _____ day.

C Fill in the blanks with the given words.

| jealous | leave | afraid | apple | ribs |

1. Adam and Eve were told not to eat an _____.

2. God took one of Adam's _____ to make Eve.

3. The snake in the Garden of Eden was a _____ animal.

4. When Adam and Eve ate the apple, they felt _____.

5. God told them to _____ the Garden of Eden.

D True or False.

1. The snake did not like to see Adam and Eve happy. T F

2. God worked all week to create the Earth. T F

3. Adam returned to Eden with his children. T F

4. The snake told Eve to eat the apple. T F

Chapter Two

Cain and Abel

🎧 7

    When Adam and Eve left Eden, they went east. Adam became a farmer[1]. Soon they had two sons. The older[2] son was named[3] Cain. The younger son was called Abel.

1. **farmer** [ˋfɑːrmər] (n.) 農夫
2. **older** [ˋɔːldər] (a.) 年紀較大的
3. **be named** （被）取名
4. **shepherd** [ˋʃepərd] (n.) 牧羊人
5. **all day long** 整天
6. **would** [wʊd] (aux.) 會
7. **follow** [ˋfɑːlou] (v.) 跟隨
8. **flock** [flɑːk] (n.) 群
9. **grow up** 長大
10. **field** [fiːld] (n.) 田地
11. **become + adj.**：變成……
　　（= **get** + 形容詞）
12. **rough** [rʌf] (a.) 粗糙的

Abel became a shepherd[4]. All day long[5] he would[6] follow[7] his flock[8] of sheep. Cain grew up[9] to be a farmer, like his father. He worked hard in the fields[10]. His hands became[11] rough[12] and dirty. He thought, "This is very difficult work. I think it's easier to be a shepherd."

One Point Lesson

◦ **I think it's** easier to be a shepherd.
　我覺得當個牧羊人比較輕鬆。

I think (that) + 主詞 + 動詞……：
這是常見的「主要句子＋從屬子句」用法

e.g. **I thought he was** in New York. 我以為他在紐約。

In Eden, Adam and Eve talked to and thanked God directly[1]. But now they had a new way. They would give precious[2] things to God. They made a fire[3] on a stone altar[4] and put the things in the fire. This way[5], they could see the gift going up to heaven in the smoke[6].

One day, Adam's family prepared their gifts to God. Abel put a fat, young lamb[7] on the altar. The flames[8] grew large. This meant that God was pleased with[9] Abel's present. Then Cain put his grains[10] and green herbs[11] on the fire. But the flames became small.

1. **directly** [də`rektli] (adv.)
   直接地；正對地

2. **precious** [`preʃəs]
   (a.) 珍貴的；寶貴的

3. **make a fire** 升火

4. **altar** [`ɑ:ltər] (n.) 祭壇

5. **this way** 如此一來；
   以這個方式（方法）

6. **smoke** [smouk] (n.) 煙

7. **lamb** [læm] (n.) 羔羊

8. **flame** [fleɪm] (n.) 火焰

9. **be pleased with . . .**
   對……滿意

10. **grain** [greɪn] (n.) 穀物

11. **herb** [ɜ:rb] (n.)
    藥草；香草（可佐食的）

Cain was angry. He saw that the Lord[1] took Abel's gift easily. But God would not accept[2] Cain's gift.

Cain told Abel to meet him in a lonely[3] field. When Abel came, Cain killed him.

God called out[4] to Cain, "Why did you kill your brother? No plants will grow for you anymore. You will move around[5] the earth to find food."

Cain replied[6], "Oh Lord, it is too much[7]. People will kill me when they see me on the street."

God said, "I will put a mark[8] on your forehead. It will be a warning[9]. If anyone kills you, I will punish[10] him. But this mark will also make people remember your crime[11]."

So Cain left his home. Some people say he went to the land of Nod.

1. **the Lord** 主；基督教義中的神（= God）
2. **accept** [əkˋsept] (v.) 接受
3. **lonely** [ˋloʊnli] (a.) 荒僻的
4. **call out** 召集；召喚
5. **move around** 居無定所；輾轉遷移
6. **reply** [rɪˋplaɪ] (v.) 回答
7. **too much** 過度的
8. **mark** [mɑːrk] (n.) 印記；標記
9. **warning** [ˋwɔːrnɪŋ] (n.) 警告
10. **punish** [ˋpʌnɪʃ] (v.) 懲罰
11. **crime** [kraɪm] (n.) 罪行

Noah's Ark[1]

God was upset[2]. Everywhere He looked, people were evil[3]. God decided He would destroy[4] everyone and everything on Earth. "I will start again," He thought.

There was only one man that God liked. His name was Noah. God came to Noah, and ordered[5] him to build a big boat. He told Noah that He would cover the Earth with water.

Noah and his sons started to work on[6] the boat. Other people laughed at him. Noah tried to warn[7] them about the flood[8], but they just laughed harder.

1. **ark** [ɑːrk] (n.) 聖經上大洪
   水時諾亞所乘逃命的方舟
   （源自拉丁文「箱子」）

2. **upset** [ʌpˋset] (a.)
   煩亂的；不高興的

3. **evil** [ˋiːvəl] (a.) 邪惡的

4. **destroy** [dɪˋstrɔɪ] (v.) 毀滅

5. **order** [ˋɔːrdər] (v.) 命令

6. **work on** 努力地工作

7. **warn** [wɔːrn] (v.) 警告

8. **flood** [flʌd] (n.) 洪水

One Point Lesson

◆ **Everywhere** he looked, people were evil.
  祂放眼望去的每一個地方，人們都是邪惡的。

---

everywhere：到處（副詞）

e.g. I looked **everywhere**, but I couldn't find my key.
  我到處都看了，可是找不到我的鑰匙。

🎧 11

Finally the boat was finished. God came to Noah and said, "Gather¹ enough food for you and your family. And bring two of every animal into² the boat."

After Noah did what God told him, it began to rain. This was a big, heavy³ rain. Soon the land was covered with⁴ water. Only Noah, his family, and the animals on the boat were alive⁵.

1. **gather** [ˋgæðər] (v.) 採集
2. **bring . . . into . . .**
   把……帶到……中
   (bring-brought-brought)
3. **heavy** [ˋhevi] (a.) 猛烈的
4. **be covered with**
   被……覆蓋

5. **alive** [əˋlaɪv] (a.) 活著的
6. **clear** [klɪr] (v.) 消散
7. **drop** [drɑːp] (v.) 落下
8. **Mount** [maʊnt] (n.) 山
   （字首大寫表示專有名詞）
9. **make a home** 建立家園

It rained for forty days and forty nights. As the clouds cleared[6], the waters began to drop.[7] After one hundred and fifty days, Noah's boat touched land.

Noah saw that they were on Mount[8] Ararat. Noah and his family made a new home[9] near the mountain. Then they gave precious gifts to God.

Tower of Babel

🎧 12

Noah had many children. Those children had more children. Soon there were thousands of[1] people again in the world.

They went around[2] the earth, looking for[3] a good place to live. Soon these people came to the valley[4] of Shinar. They found a lot of[5] clay[6] and water there.

"Let's make bricks[7]," they said.

"We can build a tall tower[8]."

"Let's build a tower all the way[9] up to[10] heaven!"

The people were very excited. They started to make many bricks and the tower rose up[11] higher and higher.

1. **thousands of** 成千上萬
2. **go around** 走遍
3. **look for** 尋找
4. **valley** 山谷；河谷
5. **a lot of** 許多的；大量的
6. **clay** [kleɪ] (n.) 泥土；黏土
7. **brick** [brɪk] (n.) 磚
8. **tower** [ˋtaʊər] (n.) 塔
9. **all the way** 一路通到（達到）；完全地
10. **up to** 達到；及於
11. **rise up** (rise-rose-risen) 升起；隆起；聳起

One Point Lesson

◦ The tower rose up **higher and higher**. 塔也越來越高聳。

形容詞比較級 + **and** + 形容詞比較級：越來越……

e.g. She became **sadder and sadder**. 她變得越來越憂傷。

39

🎧 13

One day, God looked down[1] and saw the tower. "These people have become too proud[2]," said God. "They think they can touch heaven by building bricks."

God decided to teach these people a lesson[3]. "Let's see if[4] they can work together in different languages," said God.

As soon as[5] He spoke, the people became confused[6]. They could not understand each other[7]. Everywhere, people were making strange sounds[8]. The work stopped. The people became afraid and left the valley. The tower these people built was called Babel.

Never again did all the people of the earth share[9] the same language.

1. **look down** 俯視；往下看
2. **proud** [praʊd] (a.) 驕傲的
3. **teach a lesson** 教訓
4. **see if** 看看是否……
5. **as soon as** 一……就……
6. **confused** [kən`fjuːzd] (a.) 困惑的；混淆的
7. **each other** 彼此；相互
8. **make a sound** 發出聲音
9. **share** [ʃer] (v.) 共用；分享

One Point Lesson

◆ **Never again** did all the people of the earth share the same language. 世上的人們再也沒有共同的語言。

---

never again：再也不，再也沒有；never 必用於否定句。

e.g. **Never** did I think of him. 我從未想到他。
= I never thought of him.

41

A Circle the words related to "Babel Tower."

tower

brick

herb

rise up

clay

music

soldier

language

B Fill in the blanks with proper numeric words.

God worked for _six_ days.

❶ It rained for _____ days and _____ nights.

❷ _____ of each animal were brought into Noah's boat.

❸ Noah's boat floated for _____ days after it stopped raining.

C Fill in the blanks with right tense of the given verbs.

grow	be caused	take	feel

1. The flood _____ by rain.

2. Abel _____ care of sheep.

3. Cain _____ grain.

4. Cain _____ angry with Abel.

D True or False

1. The workers on the Tower of Babel lost their voices. T F

2. God marked Cain's forehead to protect him. T F

3. Noah died on his boat, but his sons survived. T F

E Rearrange the following sentences in chronological order.

1. The people started building the Tower of Babel.

2. Noah's children grew in numbers.

3. The Earth was covered in a flood.

4. Everyone suddenly spoke a different language.

_____ ⇨ _____ ⇨ _____ ⇨ _____

Before You Read

pyramid
金字塔

Egyptian soldier
埃及士兵

They are building a pyramid.
他們正在蓋金字塔。

brick
磚塊

Pharaoh
法老

Jewish slave
猶太奴隸

Pharaoh ordered to kill all the Jewish male babies.
法老下令殺光猶太人的男嬰。

Israelite
以色列人

servant
僕人

River Nile
尼羅河

She is carrying baby Moses.
她正抱著小摩西。

male
男的

Egyptian princess
埃及公主

basket
籃

be born
出生

carry
抱

palace
皇宮

first-born
頭胎的

raise
撫養

prince
王子

grow up
長大

Moses grew up as an Egyptian prince.
摩西以王子的身分長大。

**run away
escape**
逃離;逃跑

He found out he was an Israelite.
他發現自己是以色列人。

44

Canaan 迦南

Mount Sinai
西奈山（上帝在此山
山上傳十誡給摩西）

voice
聲音
Lead your people to Canaan.
帶領你的人民到迦南。

bush
灌木叢

stay green
保持綠色

shepherd
牧羊人

rod / stick
棒：杖

hold
持：握

Moses became a shepherd.
摩西變成了牧羊人。

Pharaoh's army is chasing after
Moses and his people.
法老的大軍正緊追在摩西及其人民之後。

Moses left Egypt with the Israelites.
摩西帶著以色列人離開埃及。

Forward!
前進！

Red Sea
紅海

crowd
人群

split into two
一分為二

Dry land appeared.
露出乾燥的地面。

You shall follow these laws.
你們要遵守這些誡律。

The Ten Commandments
十誡

shout 吶喊

pray 祈禱

a golden calf
金牛

You shall have no gods but me.
你們應只信奉我一神。

punish
懲罰

camp
營區

45

Chapter Three

Moses and the Burning[1] Bush[2]

🎧 14

There came a time when the Israelites[3] moved to Egypt to find food. Eventually[4] they became the slaves[5] of Pharaoh[6].

Pharaoh was worried because they continued to grow in number. So he told his soldiers[7] to kill all the Jewish[8] male[9] babies.

1. **burning** [`bɜːrnɪŋ] (a.) 燃燒的
2. **bush** [bʊʃ] (n.) 灌木叢
3. **Israelite** [`ɪzrəlaɪt] (n.) 以色列人；猶太人
4. **eventually** [ɪ`ventʃuəli] (adv.) 最終地；末了地
5. **slave** [sleɪv] (n.) 奴隸
6. **Pharaoh** [`feroʊ] (n.) 法老王
7. **soldier** [`soʊldʒər] (n.) 士兵
8. **Jewish** [`dʒuːɪʃ] (a.) 猶太人的
9. **male** [meɪl] (a.) 男性的
10. **place** [pleɪs] (v.) 放置

Moses was born at this time to an Israelite woman in Egypt. She did not want him to be killed. She placed[10] Moses in a basket and then put the basket in the river Nile.

🎧 15

An Egyptian[1] princess found Moses and raised[2] the baby herself. Moses grew up as[3] an Egyptian prince.

Moses found out[4] that he was really an Israelite. So he ran away from Egypt and became a shepherd.

One day, a nearby[5] bush began to burn[6]. Moses was surprised because the bush stayed[7] green! When Moses came closer, he heard a voice.

1. **Egyptian** [ɪˋdʒɪpʃən] (a.) 埃及的
2. **raise** [reɪz] (v.) 扶養；養育
3. **as** [əz] (prep.) 以……身分
4. **find out** 發現
5. **nearby** [ˋnɪrbaɪ] (a.) 附近的
6. **burn** [bɜːrn] (v.) 燃燒
7. **stay + adj.** : 維持……

8. **lead** [liːd] (v.) 領導
   (lead-led-led)
9. **Canaan** (n.) 迦南地
   （聖經中的樂土）
10. **hold** [hoʊld] (v.) 持；握
    (hold-held-held)
11. **rod** [rɑːd] (n.) 竿；杖

"I am the God of the Israelites," said the voice. "I have seen the Israelites suffering in Egypt. I want you to lead[8] your people to Canaan[9]. This is a good land with milk and honey."

Moses was afraid, but he believed in God. So he left the burning bush, and started back to Egypt holding[10] the rod[11] of God.

Escape[1] from Egypt

God sent[2] nine terrible disasters[3] to Egypt but Pharaoh would not let the Israelites leave. Finally God killed all the first-born[4] Egyptians. Then Pharaoh told Moses to take his people and go from Egypt.

1. **escape** [ɪˋskeɪp] (n.) 逃亡
2. **send** [send] (v.) 派遣;降賜 (send-sent-sent)
3. **disaster** [dɪˋzæstər] (n.) 災難
4. **first-born** 第一個出生的孩子;古代多指長子
5. **change one's mind** 改變心意或主意 (mind 心智;思想)
6. **army** [ˋɑrmi] (n.) 軍隊
7. **chase after** 從後追趕
8. **shore** [ʃɔr] (n.) 岸邊
9. **the Red Sea** 紅海
10. **catch up with** 趕上;追上 (catch-caught-caught)
11. **raise** [reɪz] (v.) 舉起;抬起

"Forward!" cried Pharaoh.
Then God released[4] the
waters. They rushed[5] back
together and covered[6] the
Egyptian army. Pharaoh and
all his soldiers died. The
Israelites were safe and free.

4. **release** [rɪˋliːs] (v.)
   釋放；放開

5. **rush** [rʌʃ] (v.)
   急促地前進；衝進

6. **cover** [ˋkʌvər] (v.)
   覆蓋；淹沒

The Ten Commandments[1]

🎧 18

In the desert[2], the Israelites camped[3] near Mount Sinai. It was three months after they escaped from Egypt.

Moses told the people to wait. Then he went alone up[4] into the mountain.

God called to[5] Moses. "I want to come close to the Israelites so they can hear me. I will come in a great cloud in two days."

1. **the Ten Commandments** 聖經中的十誡（commandment 戒律）
2. **desert** [`dezərt] (n.) 沙漠
3. **camp** [kæmp] (v.) 紮營
4. **go up** 上行
5. **call to . . .** 叫喚……

6. **thunder** [`θʌndər] (n.) 雷
7. **crash** [kræʃ] (v.) 發出轟隆隆的撞擊聲
8. **frightened** [`fraɪtənd] (a.) 受驚嚇的；極害怕的
9. **the foot** 以腳來引申為物體的底部

After two days, a storm moved over Mount Sinai. Thunder[6] crashed[7] in the sky. The Israelites were frightened[8]. But Moses led them to the foot[9] of Mount Sinai.

One Point Lesson

◆ I will come in a great cloud **in two days**.
兩天內我會乘一大片烏雲來到。

---

in + 時間詞：表示在該時間所指的期限內。

e.g. He will move to this house **in a month**.
他會在一個月內搬到這棟屋子。

God spoke, "I am the Lord, your God. You shall obey[1] these laws."

You shall have no gods but[2] me.
You shall make no statues[3] or pictures of gods.
You shall not use my name carelessly[4].
Remember the Sabbath[5] day, and keep[6] it holy[7].
Honor[8] your father and mother.
You shall not commit[9] murder[10].
You shall not commit adultery[11].
You shall not steal.
You shall not lie.
You shall not be jealous of your neighbor.

These are the ten commandments that God told Moses and his people. They promised to follow[12] these laws.

1. **obey** [əˋbei] (v.) 服從；遵從 (反義詞：disobey 不服從)
2. **but (prep.)** 除了……之外
3. **statue** [ˋstætʃuː] (n.) 雕像
4. **carelessly** [ˋkerləslı] (adv.) 草率地；輕妄地；不小心地
5. **Sabbath** [ˋsæbəθ] (n.) 安息日
6. **keep + sth + adj.** : 使（保持）某人事物如何 (keep-kept-kept)
7. **holy** [ˋhouli] (a.) 神聖的
8. **honor** [ˋaːnər] (v.) 尊敬
9. **commit** [kəˋmɪt] (v.) 犯……罪
10. **murder** [ˋmɜːrdər] (n.) 殺人
11. **adultery** [əˋdʌltəri] (n.) 通姦
12. **follow** [ˋfaːlou] (v.) 遵行

One Point Lesson

◊ **You shall obey these laws.** 你們應遵從這些誡律。

shall：1. 應該（表示命令，規定）
　　　 2. 將……會……（英語常用於第一人稱，
　　　　 英美口語通常用 will 代替）

e.g. **What shall I do next?** 接下來我該怎麼做？

🎧 20

Again, God called Moses up the mountain.
This time, Moses stayed on Mount Sinai for
forty days. The people became afraid. They
asked[1] Aaron, Moses's brother, to make them a
new god.

When God saw them pray[2] before a golden
calf[3], He became very angry. Moses begged[4]
Him not to punish the Israelites. God wrote
His commandments on two stones. Moses took
these stones down to the camp.

1. **ask** + 受詞 + **to** ...
   要求⋯⋯去做⋯⋯
2. **pray** [preɪ] (v.) 祈禱;祈求
3. **calf** [kæf] (n.) 牛犢;幼獸

4. **beg** [bɛg] (v.) 懇求;乞討
5. **protect** [prə`tɛkt] (v.) 保護
6. **disobey** [dɪsə`beɪ] (v.)
   違逆;不服從

"These are the commandments from God,"
he shouted. "Follow these commandments,
and He will protect[5] you. If you disobey[6] them,
you will be destroyed."

One Point Lesson

♦ **Follow these commandments, and He will
protect you.** 奉行這些誡律，祂就會保護你。

1.「祈使句 **, and + 主詞 + will + 動詞 ...** 」：
要……，（主詞）就會……。

2.「祈使句 **, or + 主詞 + will + 動詞 ...** 」：
要……，否則（主詞）就會……。

e.g. **Get up early, or you'll miss** the school bus.
要早起啊，否則你會趕不上（錯過）校車。

A According to the Ten Commandments stated in the column below, write down the proper commandment related to each sentence.

> *You shall have no gods but me.*
> *You shall make no statues or pictures of gods.*
> *You shall not use my name carelessly.*
> *Remember the Sabbath day, and keep it holy.*
> *Honor your father and mother.*
> *You shall not commit murder.*
> *You shall not commit adultery.*
> *You shall not steal.*
> *You shall not lie.*
> *You shall not be jealous of your neighbor.*

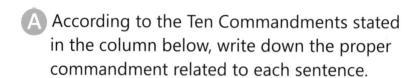

> A man secretly takes money from his friend.
> ⇨ *You shall not steal.*
> _____

❶ A man shoots a police officer to be killed.

⇨ _____

❷ A person prays to Buddha.

⇨ _____

❸ A businessman works on Sunday.

⇨ _____

❹ You hate your friend because she is beautiful.

⇨ _____

B Choose the best answer to each question.

❶ Why did God get angry at his people in the desert?

(a) They were stealing from each other.

(b) They were fighting each other.

(c) They were praying to a golden calf.

❷ What happened to Pharaoh and his army?

(a) They were killed by snakes.

(b) They drowned in the Red Sea.

(c) They got lost in the desert.

C Rearrange the following sentences in chronological order.

❶ God told Moses and his people the Ten Commandments.

❷ Moses was put in a basket on the River Nile.

❸ God sent many disasters to the Egyptians.

❹ Pharaoh let the Israelites go from Egypt.

_____ ⇨ _____ ⇨ _____ ⇨ _____

Before You Read

Tell me the secret
of your strength.
告訴我你力大無窮的秘密吧。

Samson 參孫

the strongest man 最強壯的男子
strength 力量
secret of strength 力量很大的秘密

Delilah
大利拉

pillar
柱子

rope
繩子

lie
謊言
liar
說謊者
truth
真相

fall in love with
愛上了……
Samson fell in love with Delilah.
參孫愛上了大利拉。

If my hair is cut, I will lose my strength.
把我的頭髮剪了，我就會失去力氣了。

collapse 倒塌
fall over 倒下

He pushed against
the pillars of the temple.
他用力推廟裡的柱子。

Philistine leader / official 非利士的領袖
非利士的領袖
enemy
敵人

make a plan
擬定計劃

push against
推向

temple
廟宇

war 戰爭
defeat 擊敗

on the other side of the valley
在山谷的另一頭

The stone hit Goliath in the center of his forehead.
石頭擊中了歌利亞的正前額。

forehead

David
大衛

teenager 青少年
wise 智慧的

sling
投石器

swing 揮動
throw 投擲

army
軍隊

Goliath
歌利亞

warrior
戰士

almost 10 feet tall
幾乎有10尺高

armor
盔甲

terrified
害怕的

He was covered in bronze armor.
他身著青銅製的盔甲。

spear
矛

hold up
舉起

sword
劍

Send your best warrior to fight me!
派出你們最優秀的戰士
來跟我對戰吧！

Goliath fell down on his face.
歌利亞仆倒在地。

Samson

Samson was the king of Israel for twenty years. He was also the strongest man in the world. He killed many Philistines[1], the enemies[2] of Israel.

Samson fell in love with[3] a beautiful woman named Delilah. When the Philistine leaders[4] heard this, they made a plan[5]. Some of them went to her and said, "Find the secret[6] of Samson's great strength[7], and we will pay[8] you a lot of money."

One evening, Delilah said to Samson, "What's the secret of your strength?"

Samson answered, "If someone ties me up[9] with seven new bowstrings[10], I will be as weak as any other man."

1. **Philistine** [ˈfɪlɪstiːn] (n.)
   （古代）非利士人
2. **enemy** [ˈenəmi] (n.) 敵人
3. **fall in love with . . .**
   愛上……(fall-fell-fallen)
4. **leader** [ˈliːdər] (n.)
   領袖；領導者
5. **make a plan** 擬定計畫

6. **secret** [ˈsiːkrɪt] (n.) 秘密
7. **strength** [streθ] (n.) 力量
   （尤指內在的力量）
8. **pay** [peɪ] (v.) 支付；償付
   (pay-paid-paid)
9. **tie up** 綑綁；繫縛
10. **bowstring** [ˈbaʊstrɪŋ] (n.) 弓弦

Delilah got seven new bowstrings. She tied Samson up during the night. Then she told the Philistines to come.

When Samson woke up, he broke the bowstrings easily. The Philistines ran away.

The next day, Delilah said to Samson, "I don't think you really love me. Now tell me how I can really tie you up."

Samson answered, "Tie me up with seven new ropes."

However, it turned out[1] he had lied to her again.

Delilah was getting angry[2] and she cried.

Samson told her the truth, "Here[3] is my secret. If my hair is cut, I will lose[4] my strength."

That night, she cut all of Samson's hair off[5]!

1. **turn out** 結果；原來
2. **get + adj.**：變得⋯⋯
3. **Here is . . .**：⋯⋯在這裡；這就是⋯⋯
4. **lose** [luːz] (v.) 失去；損失 (lose-lost-lost)
5. **cut off** 剪掉；斬斷

One Point Lesson

◆ **However**, it turned out he had lied to her again.
然而，原來他又再度騙了她。

however：在此處當連接副詞，用來轉換語氣。

e.g. I said no, **however**. 不過，我拒絕了。

The Philistines easily caught him and cut his eyes out with a knife. Then they put Samson in their prison[1].

The prison guards[2] often brought Samson to the temple[3]. Many Philistines would make fun of[4] him there, but they didn't notice[5] that his hair was growing back[6].

One day Samson was standing again at the temple. Samson prayed, "Oh Lord, make me strong just once more[7]. Let me make the Philistines suffer for what they did to me!"

1. **prison** [ˋprɪzən] (n.) 獄；牢
2. **guard** [gɑːrd] (n.) 守衛；警衛
3. **temple** [ˋtempəl] (n.) 寺廟
4. **make fun of** 捉弄；取笑
5. **notice** [ˋnoutɪs] (v.) 注意
6. **grow back** 長回來（指毛髮）
7. **just once more** 只要再一次
8. **push** [puʃ] (v.) 用力推
9. **against** [əˋgenst] (prep.) 對……
10. **pillar** [ˋpɪlər] (n.) 柱；柱狀物
11. **fall over** 傾倒；倒下
12. **collapse** [kəˋlæps] (v.) 倒塌；坍塌

He pushed[8] against[9] the pillars[10] of the temple. They fell over[11], and the temple collapsed[12]! Hundreds of Philistines died with Samson.

David and Goliath

The Israelites and the Philistines began[1] fighting[2] again. The strongest warrior[3] of the Philistines was named Goliath. He was almost ten feet tall! He was covered in heavy bronze[4] armor[5].

Goliath shouted at the Israelites who were on the other side of the valley. "Soldiers of Israel! Send[6] your best warrior to fight me! If he wins, we will be your slaves. But if I win[7], you will be our slaves!"

When the Israelites heard this, they were afraid. They didn't know what to do. Every day, Goliath shouted his challenge[8].

1. **begin + Ving/to . . .**
   開始某個動作 / 去做某事
   (begin-began-begun)
2. **fight** [faɪt] (v.) 打仗；爭戰
   (fight-fought-fought)
3. **warrior** [ˋwɔːrɪər] (n.) 戰士
4. **bronze** [brɑːnz] (a.) 青銅製的

5. **armor** [ˋɑːrmər] (n.) 盔甲
6. **send** [send] (v.) 派遣；打發
   (send-sent-sent)
7. **win** [wɪn] (v.) 贏；獲勝
   (win-won-won)
8. **challenge** [ˋtʃæləndʒ] (n.) 挑戰

One Point Lesson

◆ They didn't know **what to do**. 他們不知道該怎麼辦。

what + to + 動詞：要做……

e.g. I don't know **what to say**. 我不知道該（要）說什麼。

At this time, there was an Israeli[1] teenager[2] named David. He was a shepherd, not a warrior. David heard about Goliath, and decided to fight the warrior.

He thought to himself[3], "The Lord, our God protects me. He will protect me from this warrior."

He picked up[4] five large, smooth[5] stones and put them in his bag. Then he walked toward the Philistine camp.

1. **Israeli** [ɪzˋreɪli] (a.) 以色列人的（= Israelite）
2. **teenager** [ˋtiːnɔidʒər] (n.) 青少年
3. **think to oneself** 在心裡想
4. **pick up** 拾起；撿起
5. **smooth** [smuð] (a.) 光滑的；圓滑的
6. **silly** [ˋsɪli] (a.) 愚蠢的
7. **spear** [spɪr] (n.) 槍；矛

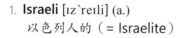

Goliath saw David coming and was angry. "Who is this boy that the Israelites send to fight me? Do they think this is a silly[6] game? I will kill you and show your head to them on my spear[7]!"

Goliath yelled and ran at David. David stood still[1] and took a stone out of[2] his bag. He put the stone in his sling[3]. Then he began to swing[4] the sling over his head.

Suddenly, he let the stone fly out of the sling. It hit Goliath right in the center of[5] his forehead! Goliath fell down on his face.

1. **stand still** 站著不動 (stand-stood-stood)
2. **out of . . .** 脫離 (……的狀態)
3. **sling** [slɪŋ] (n.) 古代的投石器（彈弓）
4. **swing** [swɪŋ] (v.) 揮動 (swing-swang-swung)
5. **in the center of . . .** : ……的中心

David ran to him and pulled Goliath's sword[6] out. David cut off Goliath's head and held it up[7] to show the Philistines.

The Philistines saw their hero's[8] head in the hand of David. They were terrified[9]. They turned and ran away. Much later[10], David became King of Israel.

6. **sword** [sɔːrd] (n.) 劍
7. **hold up** 舉起
   (hold-held-held)
8. **hero** [ˋhɪroʊ] (n.) 英雄
9. **terrified** [ˋterɪfaɪd] (a.)
   嚇壞了；受驚嚇的
10. **much later** 很久以後；事隔許久

A Fill in the name of the person who fits the description.

David   Delilah   Samson   Goliath

1 A long-haired strong man : _____

2 The strongest warrior of the Philistines : _____

3 A teenage shepherd who became a hero : _____

4 A woman who Samson fell in love with : _____

B Fill in the blanks with the given words.

> warrior   challenge   pillars   sling

1 Goliath shouted his _____ every morning.

2 David was a shepherd, not a _____.

3 Samson pushed against the _____ of the temple.

4 David threw a stone at Goliath with a _____.

C Choose the right answer to each question.

1 Why did Delilah trick Samson?

(a) Because she was a Philistine.

(b) Because the Philistines said they would kill her.

(c) Because she wanted money.

2 **What did he become when David grew up?**

(a) A shepherd.

(b) A warrior.

(c) A king.

D True or False.

1 David's stone hit Goliath in the forehead. T F

2 Delilah really loved Samson. T F

3 David fought Goliath with a sword. T F

4 Samson was the strongest man. T F

Chapter Five

King Solomon

🎧 27

    When David died, his son, Solomon became King. One day, two women came before Solomon. They wanted him to solve[1] their argument[2]. One of them was carrying[3] a baby.

    The first woman said, "King Solomon, listen to our story. This woman and I both had babies. One night, this woman's baby died. She took her dead baby into my room. As[4] I was sleeping, she took my baby!"

    "Liar[5]!" shouted the other woman. "Your story is not true!"

---

1. **solve** [sɑːlv] (v.) 解決（疑難；問題）
2. **argument** [`ɑːrgjəmənt] (n.) 爭論；爭執
3. **carry** [`kæri] (v.) 抱；攜帶
4. **as** (conj.) 當……之時
5. **liar** [`laɪər] (n.) 騙子；說謊的人

King Solomon shouted, "Cut the baby into two with a sword. Then give one half to each woman. This way, they will both be satisfied[1]."

"No!" cried the first woman. "Let her have the baby. It's better that I lose him and he lives."

The second woman cried out, "That is a good decision[2]."

When King Solomon heard these words, he said to the first woman, "You must be the true mother of this baby. No mother would allow[3] her baby to be killed."

When the people heard this judgment[4], they knew their king was wise[5] and good.

1. **satisfied** [ˈsætɪsfaɪd] (a.) 滿足的；滿意的
2. **decision** [dɪˈsɪʒən] (n.) 決定
3. **allow sb to . . .**：容許某人做……
4. **judgment** [ˈdʒʌdʒmənt] (n.) 判斷；裁判
5. **wise** [waɪz] (a.) 智慧的；睿智的

Daniel and the Lions

 29

   Daniel was a Jewish[1] prisoner[2] taken from
Jerusalem[3]. Persia had defeated[4] Israel in war.
The Persian king wanted many young Jews[5] to
serve[6] him. Daniel was one of these young men.

   When Daniel grew up, a new King took
power[7] in Persia. His name was Darius. King
Darius really liked Daniel. Daniel was now a
very wise and good man. So Darius made Daniel
the most important official[8] in Persia.

1. **Jewish** [`dʒu:ɪʃ] (a.)
   猶太人的；猶太教的
2. **prisoner** [`prɪzənər] (n.) 犯人
3. **Jerusalem** [dʒəˋru:sələm] (n.)
   耶路撒冷
4. **defeat** [dɪˋfi:t] (v.) 打敗

5. **Jew** [dʒu:] (n.) 猶太人
6. **serve** [sɜːrv] (v.) 服侍
7. **take power** 當政；掌權
8. **official** [əˋfɪʃəl] (n.) 官員
9. **find fault with sb**
   挑某人毛病

Many of the other Persian officials were jealous of Daniel. They tried to think of some way to make Darius angry with Daniel. But Daniel was a very honest man. His enemies could not find any fault with⁹ Daniel.

One Point Lesson

◈ Persia **had defeated** Israel in war.
波斯在戰爭中打敗了以色列。

had + 過去分詞：過去完成式，用來表示在過去的某個時間點已經發生的事。（常用於敘述故事時）

e.g. The train **had** already **left** when I went to the station.
我去車站時，火車已經開走了。

30

But one day, a Persian official had an idea[1].
All the officials went to King Darius.

They told Darius that there was a lot of
confusion[2] in Persia. "The people are asking
many different gods many different things,"
they said. "You should make a new law. No one
should be permitted[3] to pray for the next
thirty days."

"What will happen if a man is caught[4]
praying?" asked King Darius.

"Then he should be thrown[5] into the cave[6]
where the lions are kept[7]," answered the
officials.

King Darius signed[8] the new law. When
Daniel heard about the new law, he was sad but
he couldn't stop praying. He went to his room
to pray to God. The officials saw this and told
the King. Darius ordered the arrest[9] of Daniel.

1. **idea** [aɪ`dɪə] (n.) 主意；構想
2. **confusion** [kən`fjuːʒən] (n.) 混亂
3. **permit** [pər`mɪt] (v.) 准許；容許
   (permit-permitted-permitted)
4. **catch** [kætʃ] (v.) 無意間發現
5. **throw** [θroʊ] (v.) 扔；拋；擲
   (throw-threw-thrown)
6. **cave** [keɪv] (n.) 洞穴
7. **keep** [kiːp] (v.) 養（牲口、貓、
   狗等）；拘禁 (keep-kept-kept)
8. **sign** [saɪn] (v.) 簽字；簽署
9. **arrest** [ə`rest] (v.) 逮捕；拘捕

31

Daniel was taken to the lion's cave. The king said, "Your God will find a way to save[1] you. I cannot."

Then the guards put Daniel into the cave. They closed the opening[2] with a large rock. King Darius was so sad that he could not eat, drink or sleep. In the morning, he ran to the cave. There stood Daniel, unhurt[3]! King Darius was amazed[4].

Daniel said, "My Lord sent an angel[5] to shut[6] the mouths of the lions."

Then King Darius knew the power of Daniel's God.

1. **save** [seɪv] (v.) 解救;拯救
2. **opening** [`oupənɪŋ] (n.) 開口處;出入口
3. **unhurt** [ʌn`hɜ:rt] (a.) 未受傷的
4. **amazed** [ə`meɪzd] (a.) 驚異的;驚嘆的
5. **angel** [`eɪndʒəl] (n.) 天使
6. **shut** [ʃʌt] (v.) 關閉 (shut-shut-shut)

King Darius was **so sad that** he could not eat, drink or sleep. 大流士王難過得吃不下，喝不下，也睡不著。

so + 形容詞 + that：如此……以致於……

e.g. He was **so tired that** he could not walk.
他累得走不動了。

A Circle the words best describe King Solomon.

liar

judgment

foolish

wise

young

David's son

cruel

B Fill in the blanks with the given words using the present perfect tense.

make   order   throw   solve

❶ The guards _____ Daniel into the lions' cave.

❷ Solomon _____ the argument between the two women.

❸ King Solomon _____ a good decision.

❹ Darius _____ the arrest of Daniel.

C Choose the right answer to each question.

① **How did Solomon know who the real mother was?**

(a) God told him.

(b) The real mother didn't want her baby to be killed.

(c) He cut the baby into two parts.

② **Why didn't the lions eat Daniel?**

(a) because they weren't hungry.

(b) because god sent an angel

to protect him.

(c) because daniel killed

the lions with his hands.

D True or False.

① Solomon really wanted to kill the baby.　　T　F

② The officials were jealous of Daniel.　　T　F

③ King Darius signed a law that Daniel　　T　F
didn't like.

④ Daniel was born in Persia.　　T　F

Appendixes

1 Basic Grammar

2 Guide to Listening Comprehension

3 Listening Guide

4 Listening Comprehension

1

Basic Grammar

要增強英文閱讀理解能力，應練習找出英文的主結構。
要擁有良好的英語閱讀能力，首先要理解英文的段落結構。

「英文的主要句型結構比較簡單」

所有的英語句子都是由主詞和動詞所構成的，不管句子再怎麼長或複雜，它的架構一定是「主詞和動詞」，而「補語」和「受詞」是做補充主詞和動詞的角色。

主詞	動詞
某樣東西（人、事、物）	如何做

He runs (very fast).
他　跑步（非常快）。

It is raining.
天　下著雨。

主詞	動詞	補語	（補充的話）
某樣東西（人、事、物）	如何做	怎麼樣	

This is a cat.
這　是　一隻貓。

The cat is very big.
這隻貓　是　非常大。

主詞　　　動詞　　　受詞

某樣東西　　如何做　　什麼
（人、事、物）

人，事物，
兩者皆是受詞

I **like** **you** .
我 喜歡 妳。

You **gave** **me** some flowers .
妳 給了 我 一些花。

主詞　　　動詞　　　受詞　　補語

某樣東西　　如何做　　什麼　怎麼樣／什麼
（人、事、物）

You **make** **me** happy .
妳 使 我 快樂。

I **saw** **him** running .
我 看見 他 在跑步。

　　　其他修飾語或副詞等，都可以視為為了完成句子而臨時、額外、特別附加的，閱讀起來便可更加輕鬆；先具備這些基本概念，再閱讀《聖經故事》的部分精選篇章，最後做了解文章整體架構的練習。

In the beginning there **was** **only God** .
　　　　　最初　　　　是　　只有神。

He **created** **the earth** .
祂 創造了 地球。

The earth **was** **dark** and **covered** with water.
地球 是 黑暗的 而且 覆蓋 被水

So **God** **said** , " **Let there be** **light** ".
於是 神 說 讓（世上）有 光亮。

Light covered the Earth . God liked it .
光明　　壟罩　　地球。　　神　　喜歡　　它（這安排）。

He called the light , " day ".
祂　　叫　　光明　　「晝」。

He called the dark , " night ".
祂　　稱　　黑暗　　「夜」。

On the second day, God created the sky .
在第二天，　　神　　創造了　　天空。

Now the world had two parts .
現在 世界（宇宙）有了　　兩個部分。

One was the earth . The other was the heavens .
一個 是　　地面。　另一個　是　　天空。

On the fourth day, God said , " Day must be divided from night."
第四天，　　神　說：「白晝 必須　　被區隔　　與夜晚。」

So He made the sun and the moon .
於是，祂 創造了　　太陽和月亮。

Then God put stars and planets in the sky.
接著，神　　擺放 大大小小的群星　　在天空裡。

On the fifth day, God said ,
第五天，　　神　　說：

" Let there be fish in the sea and birds in the air."
「讓有　　魚　在海中，而且　鳥　在　空中。」

God blessed all kinds of fish and birds.
神　　賜福　　所有的魚類和鳥禽。

" Live well and have many children ."
「活得 好好地，而且　　多子多孫。」

On the sixth day, God created all the animals .
第六天， 神 創造了 所有的動物。

Some animals ran fast over the grass.
有些動物 奔跑 快速地 在草地上。

And some animals hid in the trees.
有些動物 躲藏 在樹林間。

God looked at the animals he created.
神 望著 動物們 祂所創造的。

He was happy .
祂 是 開心的。

Then God said , "I will make a man and a woman .
然後 神 說：「我要 創造 一個男人和一個女人。

They will rule over all the animals on land.
他們 將 統治 所有動物 在陸地上的。」

God rested on the seventh day.
神 休息 在第七天。

He blessed this day , and made it His special day .
祂 賜福 這一天， 並且 訂 這天 為祂的特別日。

This is why man does not work on this day .
這 是 為什麼人們在這一天不工作（的原因）。

Guide to Listening Comprehension

 Use your book's CD to enjoy the audio version. When listening to the story, use some of the techniques shown below. If you take time to study some phonetic characteristics of English, listening will be easier.

Get in the flow of English.

English creates a rhythm formed by combinations of strong and weak stress intonations. Each word has its particular stress that combines with other words to form the overall pattern of stress or rhythm In a particular sentence.

When speaking and listening to English, it is essential to get in the flow of the rhythm of English. It takes a lot of practice to get used to such a rhythm. So, you need to start by identifying the stressed syllable in a word.

Listen for the strongly stressed words and phrases.

In English, key words and phrases that are essential to the meaning of a sentence are stressed louder. Therefore, pay attention to the words stressed with a higher pitch. When listening to an English recording for the first time, what matters most is to listen for a general understanding of what you hear. Do not try to hear every single word. Most of the unstressed words are articles or auxiliary verbs, which don't play an important role in the general context. At this level, you can ignore them.

Pay attention to liaisons.

In reading English, words are written with a space between them. There isn't such an obvious guide when it comes to listening to English. In oral English, there are many cases when the sounds of words are linked with adjacent words.

For instance, let's think about the phrase "**take off**," which can be used in "take off your clothes." "Take off your clothes" doesn't sound like [teɪk ɔːf] with each of the words completely and clearly separated from the others. Instead, it sounds as if almost all the words in context are slurred together, [ˈteɪkɔːf], for a more natural sound.

Shadow the voice of the native speaker.

Finally, you need to mimic the voice of the native speaker. Once you are sure you know how to pronounce all the words in a sentence, try to repeat them like an echo. Listen to the book again, but this time you should try a fun exercise while listening to the English.

This exercise is called "shadowing." The word "shadow" means a dark shade that is formed on a surface. When used as a verb, the word refers to the action of following someone or something like a shadow. In this exercise, pretend you are a parrot and try to shadow the voice of the native speaker.

Try to mimic the reader's voice by speaking at the same speed, with the same strong and weak stresses on words, and pausing or stopping at the same points.

Experts have already proven this technique to be effective. If you practice this shadowing exercise, your English speaking and listening skills will improve by leaps and bounds. While shadowing the native speaker, don't forget to pay attention to the meaning of each phrase and sentence.

Step 1 Listen to what you want to shadow many times. Start out by just trying to shadow a few words or a sentence.

 Step 2 Mimic the CD out loud. You can shadow everything the speaker says as if you are singing a round, or you also can speak simultaneously with the recorded voice of the native speaker.

 Step 3 As you practice more, try to shadow more. For instance, shadow a whole sentence or paragraph instead of just a few words.

Listening Guide

Bible Stories

Chapter One page 14 🎧32

In the beginning there was only God. He (❶) (　)
earth. The earth was dark and covered with (❷). So
God said, "Let there be light." Light (❸) (　) earth.
God liked it. He called the light "day." He called the dark
"night."

❶ **created the:** 字尾的 ed 發短母音 /ɪd/。注意：the 的 e 要發短音
/ɪ/，因為後面接續的 earth 字首是母音。

❷ **water:** water 的 a 要發成半個 o。

❸ **covered the:** covered 字尾的 ed 只發 /d/。此外，the 的字尾 e
要發音，理由與 ❶ 相同。

一開始若能聽清楚發音，之後就沒有聽力的負擔。首先，請聽過摘錄的章節，之後再反覆聆聽括弧內單字的發音，並仔細閱讀各種發音的說明。以下都是以英語的典型發音為基礎，所做的簡易說明，即使這裡未提到的發音，也可以配合音檔反覆聆聽，如此一來聽力必能更上層樓。

Chapter Two pages 28–29 🎧33

When Adam and Eve left (❶), they went east. Adam became a farmer. Soon they had two sons. The older son was named Cain. The younger son was called Abel. Abel became a shepherd. All day long he (❷) ( ) his flock of sheep. Cain grew up to be a farmer, (❸) ( ) father. He worked hard in the fields. His hands became rough and dirty.

❶ **Eden:** Eden 字中第一個 e 發原音，第二個 e 發弱化的母音 /ə/。英美語發音法中，有一個多數情況皆適用的通則，就是從字母 e 開始倒數的第三個字母若為母音，則多半發原音。

❷ **would follow:** would 一字發音與 could 和 should 非常類似。字中的 oul，ou 的發音為 /u/，而 l 不發音。

❸ **like his:** his 一字要輕讀，i 發短音 /ɪ/，s 發音是 /z/。

Chapter Three page 46 `34`

There came a time when the Israelites (❶) (   ) Egypt to find food. Eventually they became the (❷) (   ) Pharaoh. Pharaoh was worried because they (❸) to grow in number. So he told his soldiers to kill all the Jewish male babies.

❶ **moved to:** moved 字尾 ed 的 e 不發音；而 d 連接下一個字 to，因為 d 與 t 為近似音，故而常省略 t 的發音。

❷ **slaves of:** slaves 中的複數 s 發音為 /z/，而 e 不發音。of 一字由於發弱音，因此常被聽錯、唸錯。of 的 o 發ㄜ音 /ə/，而 f 發音為 /v/。

❸ **continued:** continued 共有 3 個音節。3 個音節以上的字，重音大多放在第 2（例如此字）或第 3 音節上，只有少數以第 1 音節為重音（如 beautiful）。

Chapter Four pages 64–65 `35`

Samson was the king of Israel for (❶)(   ). He was also the (❷) man in the world. He killed many Philistines, the enemies of Israel. Samson fell in love with a beautiful woman named Delilah. When the Philistine leaders heard this, they (❸)(   ) plan.

❶ twenty years: twenty 一字要注意 nt 兩音的銜接是輕巧的，與 Internet 一字中的 nt 不同，Internet 的 t 發音較清楚。此外要注意 years 中的 s 發音為 /z/。

❷ strongest: strongest 字尾的 est 發弱音，所以無論聽或說時都要注意。尤其 st 都是氣音（無聲音），銜接下一個字時，要含在嘴裡唸出來。

❸ made a: made 一字發音如前述，從字母 e 開始倒數的第三個字母若為母音，則多發原音。

Chapter Five page 78 🎧 36

> When David died, his son Solomon became King. One day, two women came before Solomon. They (❶) ( ) to solve their argument. One of them was carrying a baby. The first woman said, "King Solomon, listen to our (❷). This woman and I both had babies. One night, this woman's baby died. She took her (❸) ( ) into my room. As I was sleeping, she took my baby!"

❶ wanted him: wanted 字尾 ed 發短母音 /ɪd/。銜接 him 時，h 幾乎不發音。同樣的，銜接 his/her/he 等字首 h 發音的字時，h 多半幾乎不發音，除非作強調語氣時。

❷ story: story 一字要注意字首的 st。當字首為兩個相連的無聲子音時，第二個無聲子音的讀音要變成有聲音。例如 st 唸作 /sd/，sp 唸作 /sb/，sk 唸作 /sg/。

❸ dead baby: dead 一字的 ea 發短母音，銜接下一個字 baby 時，dead 的字尾 d 發音變得很輕，同樣要含在嘴裡唸它。

Listening Comprehension

🎧 37 **A** Listen to the CD and write the numbers 1, 2, 3, or 4 to the correct person who is described in each sentence.

Adam	David	Moses	Samson
_____	_____	_____	_____

🎧 38 **B** True or false.

T F ① ....

T F ② ....

🎧 39 **C** Listen to the CD and fill in the blanks.

❶ God _____ the Earth in six days.

❷ Moses asked Pharaoh to _____ his people _____.

❸ Samson _____ that the baby be cut in two.

🎧 40 **D** Listen to the CD. Write down the question you hear, and choose the correct answer.

1 _____?

(a) Because they didn't have enough water.

(b) Because they suddenly spoke different languages.

(c) Because there was a flood.

2 _____?

(a) Moses

(b) Daniel

(c) Cain

🎧 41 **E** Listen to the CD and choose the correct answer.

1 _____ •

2 _____ •

3 _____ •

• a because they ate the apple.

• b because he was jealous.

• c by ordering the baby to be killed.

Translation

簡介

《聖經》的起源和意義

p. 4 「Holy Bible」的字源來自希臘文的「Biblion」，這個字被直接翻譯為「book」，但是到了十二世紀，變成了「Holy Bible」。

《聖經》有兩個部分：《舊約聖經》和《新約聖經》。《舊約聖經》是上帝透過摩西的締結和平，和以色列人所做的聖約。《新約聖經》則是透過耶穌的教語，來宣揚基督教的教義。

新舊約聖經合計共 66 卷，所集結的文章作者超過四十位，時間上跨越了一千五百多年。這些書卷內容記載了大量的各個時期的歷史和基督教的教義。

《舊約聖經》一開始是講創世，接著講到亞當和夏娃、亞伯拉罕家族、摩西、猶太人逃出埃及，講述了人類的歷史。其中也講到了以色列諸王和以利亞先知、但以理先知等等。

《舊約聖經》的人物

亞當	上帝所創造的第一個人類，按照神的形象而造，生存於地上。在古希伯來文，「Adam」有「地」的意思。
夏娃	第一個被創造的女人，由亞當的一根肋骨所造。夏娃偷嚐禁果，這成了原罪。上帝因此要求男人要工作養家，要求女人要承擔艱苦的生育任務。
摩西	帶領埃及的以色列人奴隸逃出埃及，來到應許之地。
大衛	從小擔任牧羊人，使用甩石殺死巨人歌利亞，因而聞名。後來成為以色列的第二任國王，治國輝煌。
所羅門	大衛之子，以色列的第三任國王。以睿智而聞名，曾運用自己的智慧，判別出一個新生兒的親生母親。所羅門成功統治了四十年，顯示了他的才智、能力和治政才能。
但以理	希伯來先知，「但以理」這個名字的意思是「神是我的審判者」。他對抗其他宗教的擾亂和陰謀。但以理維護了神的律法，多神教的大流士王受到他的感化，非常尊崇他。

[第一章]　創世

p. 14　萬物之初，宇宙間只有神。祂創造了地球。當時地球一片黑暗，整個被水覆蓋。於是神說：「讓世上有光亮吧。」於是光明籠罩地球。神喜歡這安排。祂把光明叫作「晝」。祂又把黑暗稱作「夜」。

第二天，神創造了天空，這下子世界有了兩個部分。一個是地面，另一個是天空。

p. 16　第三天，神將水推到一邊。乾燥的土地升了上來。神把土地稱作「陸」，把水稱作「海」。接著，神又創造了所有的植物。祂覺得這安排很好。

第四天，神說：「必須把白晝跟夜晚區隔開來。」於是，祂又創造了太陽和月亮。接著，神又將大大小小的群星放到天空裡。

第五天，神說：「讓海中有魚，空中有鳥吧。」神賜福所有的魚類和鳥禽。「好好地活著，而且要多子多孫。」

p. 18　第六天，神創造了所有的動物，有些動物在草地上奔馳，有些動物躲藏在樹林間。神望著祂所創造的動物們，祂很開心。然後神說：「我要創造一個男人和一個女人。他們會統治所有陸地上的動物。」

第七天，神休息了。祂賜福這一天，並且把這一天訂作祂的特別日。這就是為什麼人們在這一天不工作的原因。

亞當與夏娃

p. 20–21　神創造男人時，他給他取名「亞當」。神覺得亞當需要一個生活的地方。於是祂創造了一座美麗的花園，叫做「伊甸園」。

在花園中，神安置了一株特殊的蘋果樹。祂對亞當說：「切

勿吃我這株奇特之樹的果
實。如果你吃了那些蘋
果，你就會體驗到善與
惡。而且，你會變老而
死亡。」

　　有一天，神看出亞
當很孤單。「我要給這
個男人一個幫手。」於
是，趁亞當睡著時，神取走他的一根肋骨。以這根肋骨，祂創造
了一個女人。

　　亞當醒來看見夏娃，很驚喜。他感謝神。亞當和夏娃在伊甸
園中生活了很久很久，他們沒有任何苦痛或匱乏。

`p. 22-23` 伊甸園中住著一條蛇。蛇是善妒的動物。牠不高興看到
亞當和夏娃這麼快樂。

　　這一天，蛇跟夏娃說：「你們為什麼不吃那株樹上的蘋果？」

　　「我們不能吃。」夏娃說，「我們如果吃了果實，就會死掉。」

　　「聽我說，」蛇說道，「神創造了你們。祂何苦要你們死掉？
如果你們吃了果實，就會跟神一樣萬能。」

　　夏娃相信了蛇的話。她摘下一顆蘋果，咬了一口。然後把蘋
果拿給亞當。亞當也吃了蘋果。突然，亞當和夏娃感到又冷又害
怕。

`p. 24` 神見到亞當和夏娃時，就知道他們吃了那株樹上的蘋果。
「你們做了什麼？」

　　夏娃說：「蛇用計騙了我，牠告訴我說，我可以吃果實。」

　　這下子神盛怒了。「離開這裡，」祂對他們說：「你們違背
了我。現在你們必須辛苦工作來換得食物。你們會體驗痛苦和悲
傷。你們還會老去，死亡。」

　　亞當和夏娃離開了伊甸園，永遠不得返回。

［第二章］　該隱與亞伯

p. 28-29 亞當和夏娃離開伊甸園後，他們去了東方。亞當成了農夫。不久，他倆有了兩個兒子。長子取名該隱，幼子叫作亞伯。

　　亞伯當了牧羊人。他會整天趕著他的羊群。該隱長大當了農夫，克紹箕裘。他在田裡辛勤工作，雙手變得粗糙又髒污。他心想，「這個工作好辛苦。我覺得當個牧羊人比較輕鬆。」

p. 30 在伊甸園時，亞當和夏娃跟神說話和感謝神都是當面直接表示。但是現在他們用新的方式來表達。他們要將珍貴的東西送給神。他們在石砌的聖壇上升起火，將珍物放進火堆。如此一來，他們可以看著獻禮在煙霧中升向天堂。

　　這一天，亞當一家人準備著要獻給神的禮物。亞伯將一隻肥嫩的羔羊放到聖壇上。火焰變得熾旺起來。這意味神滿意亞伯送的禮物。接著該隱將自己栽種的穀物和香草放到火堆上。但是火焰卻變得微弱了。

p. 32-33 該隱心懷憤懣，他覺得神輕鬆無慮地接受了亞伯的禮物，卻不願接受該隱的禮物。

　　該隱叫亞伯到一片荒僻的田野與他碰面。當亞伯來到時，該隱殺死了他。

　　神召喚該隱，「你為什麼殺死你的弟弟？再也不會有植物生長來供你食用了。你將在人間四處流離尋覓食物。」

該隱回答，「喔神啊，這（懲罰）太嚴厲了。人們在街上看見我會殺了我啊。」

神說，「我要在你的額頭上留一個印記。它將是一個警示。假使有誰殺死你，我就會懲罰他。但是這個印記也會讓人們記得你的罪行。」

於是該隱離開了他的家。有些人說，他去了諾得之地。

諾亞方舟

p. 34 神煩亂不樂。祂放眼望去，人們到處是邪惡的。祂決定毀滅地球上的眾生萬物。「我要重新來過。」祂心想。

神喜歡的人只有一個。他名叫諾亞。神來到諾亞面前，吩咐他建造一艘大船。祂告訴諾亞，祂要使水淹沒地球。

諾亞和他的兒子們開始建造大船。別人都嘲笑他。諾亞試圖警告他們洪水將至，但是他們只是變本加厲地嘲笑。

p. 36-37 終於，大船竣工了。神來到諾亞面前，說：「集聚足夠你和你們一家人吃的食物，並且將每一種動物帶一對到船上。」

諾亞遵照神的吩咐做了之後，天開始下雨了。那是滂沱大雨。沒多久，陸地完全被水淹沒。只有諾亞、他的家人，還有帶到船上的動物倖存。

雨下了四十天四十夜。烏雲散去，海水開始下降。經過了一百五十天，諾亞的方舟觸及陸地。

諾亞看出他們是在亞拉臘山上。他和家人就在近山處建立了新的家園。然後他們向神獻上珍貴的禮物。

巴別塔

p. 38 諾亞兒女眾多。這些兒女繁衍了更多子孫。沒多久，世界上再度有了成千上萬的人。

他們走遍世界，尋覓一個美好的安身之所。不久，這些人來到示拿地山谷。他們在那裡發現大量的泥土和水。

「我們來製作磚塊吧，」他們說。

「我們可以建造一座高塔。」

「我們來建造一座直達天堂的高塔！」

人們興奮極了。他們著手製做許許多多的磚塊，塔也越來越高聳。

p. 40 這一天，神俯視人間，看見了高塔。「這些人變得太驕傲了，」神說道，「他們以為靠堆砌磚塊就能觸碰到天堂。」

神決定要教訓這些人，「我們來看看他們用不同的語言是否能攜手合作，」神說道。

祂一這麼說，人們立刻變得混亂困惑了。他們聽不懂彼此的話。到處的人都發出奇怪的聲音。工作停了下來。人們變得害怕，離開了山谷。這些人建造的高塔叫作巴別塔。

從此，世上的人們再也沒有共用的語言。

［第三章］
摩西與燃燒的叢林

p. 46-47 有一段時期，以色列人移徙至埃及尋覓食物。到最後他們成了法老王的奴隸。

法老王很憂心，因為他們的人數日增。於是他吩咐他的士兵們，殺光所有的以色列男嬰。

摩西就是在這個時候，為一個住在埃及的以色列婦女所生。她不願摩西被殺死，就把摩西安置在一個籃子裡，然後將籃子放到尼羅河上。

p. 48-49 一位埃及公主發現了摩西，便親自養育這個嬰兒。摩西以埃及王子的身分長大。

摩西調查發現，他其實是以色列人。於是他逃出埃及，成了一個牧羊人。

一天，附近一片灌木叢林燒了起來。摩西很訝異，因為那片叢林一直是青翠盎然啊！摩西靠近它時，他聽到一個聲音。

「我是以色列人的神，」那個聲音說：「我已看見以色列人在埃及受磨難。我要你帶領你的族人去迦南地。那是一片有牛奶和蜂蜜的豐美土地。」

摩西心裡害怕，但是他相信神。於是他離開了燃燒的叢林，手握著神杖啟程返回埃及。

出埃及記

p. 50–51 神對埃及降下九場可怕的災難，
但是法老王不肯放以色列人離去。最後，
神殺死了所有埃及人的長子。法老王這才
叫摩西帶著他的族人，離開埃及。

　　他們離開後，法老王又改變了主意。他召
集了一支小規模的軍隊，追趕摩西和他的族人。

　　到達紅海岸邊時，埃及的軍隊已幾乎追上他
們。這時以色列人害怕了。

　　「你是帶領我們到這裡送死嗎？」他們問摩西，「法老王率
領著一隻軍隊追來了。他會把我們全部殺光！」

　　「不要擔心，」摩西說，他舉起他的神杖：「神會將海水分開。
然後我們就能逃離了。」

p. 52–53 突然間，紅海的水一分為二。乾燥的陸地出現在兩堵水牆
之間。

　　以色列人向前飛奔。當法老王來到紅海時，以色列人已經抵
達對岸。

　　「追上去！」法老王喝令。這時，神釋放海水。兩股海水奔
湧匯合，將埃及軍隊淹沒。法老王和他的士兵們全部被淹死。以
色列人安全了，自由了。

十誡

p. 54–55 沙漠中，以色列人在西奈山附近落腳紮營。這時距離他們逃離埃及已有三個月。

摩西交代族人等待，然後他獨自登上西奈山中。

神召喚摩西：「我想要靠近以色列人，好讓他們聽得到我。兩天內我會乘一大片烏雲來到。」

過了兩天，一場暴風移至西奈山上空。雷鳴隆隆劃破天際。以色列人嚇壞了。但是摩西帶領他們來到西奈山腳下。

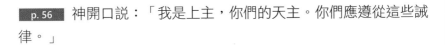

p. 56 神開口說：「我是上主，你們的天主。你們應遵從這些誡律。」

除我之外，不可有別的神。
不可製造任何神祇的雕像或畫像。
不可妄呼我的名。
要記住安息日，保持聖潔。
要孝敬父母。
不可殺人。
不可姦淫。
不可偷盜。
不可說謊。
不可忌妒你的鄰人。

這些就是神告訴摩西和他的族人的十誡。他們承諾奉行這些律法。

p. 58–59 神再度把摩西召喚到山上。這一回，摩西在西奈山上待了四十天。族人終於害怕了。他們要求亞倫，摩西的哥哥，給他們做一個新的神。

神看見他們對著一尊金色牛犢像祈禱，祂勃然大怒。摩西懇求祂不要懲罰以色列人。神將祂的誡律寫在兩塊石頭上。摩西帶著兩塊石頭下山回到營地。

「這些是神下的誡律，」他喊道：「奉行這些誡律，祂就會保護你。如果違反十誡，你將遭受毀滅。」

［第四章］ 大力士參孫

p. 64–65 參孫當了二十年的以色列王。他也是世界上最強壯的人。他殺死了無數非利士人，他們是以色列的敵人。

參孫愛上了一個美麗的女子，名叫大利拉。非利士人的領袖們聽聞此事後，他們便擬定了一個計畫。其中幾個領袖去找她說道：「查出參孫力大無窮的奧秘，我們就會付妳一大筆錢。」

一天晚間，大利拉對參孫說：「你力大無窮的奧秘是什麼？」

參孫回答：「要是有人用七條新的弓弦把我綑綁起來，我就會跟任何人一樣軟弱無力。

p. 66–67 大利拉弄到七條新的弓弦。她在夜間把參孫綑綁起來。然後她叫非利士人趕來。

參孫醒來後，他輕而易舉地掙斷弓弦。非利士人趕緊逃走。

翌日，大利拉跟參孫說：「我不認為你真心愛我。快告訴我如何才能真正把你綁起來。」

參孫回答：「用七條新的繩索把我綁起來。」

然而，他又再度騙了她。

大利拉生氣了，她哭了起來。

參孫便跟她說了實話：「我的秘密是這樣的。如果我的頭髮被剪了，我就會力氣盡失。」

那天夜裡，她把參孫的頭髮剪得精光！

p. 68–69 非利士人輕而易舉地捉住了他，還用刀子剜去他的眼睛。然後他們把參孫關入他們的監牢。

獄卒們經常把參孫帶到寺廟，許多非利士人會在那兒捉弄他，但是他們沒有注意到，他的頭髮漸漸長回來了。

一天，參孫再度站在寺廟前，參孫祈禱：「喔，主啊，只讓我再一次強壯起來吧。讓我使非利士人為他們對我做的事受罰！」

他用力推寺廟的柱子。柱子倒下，寺廟傾塌！數百名非利士人跟參孫一起被壓死。

大衛與歌利亞

p. 70-71 以色列人與非利士人再度開始交戰。非利士人當中最強健的勇士名叫歌利亞。他身高將近十呎！他全身披佩厚重的青銅甲冑。

歌利亞衝著山谷對面的以色列人吶喊：「以色列的士兵們！派出你們最優秀的勇士來跟我對戰！假如他戰勝了，我們就當你們的奴隸。但是如果我贏了，你們就要當我們的奴隸！」

以色列人聽到此話，他們害怕了。他們不知道該怎麼辦。歌利亞天天喊著他的挑戰。

p. 72-73 當時，有一個以色列少年，名叫大衛。他是個牧羊人，不是戰士。大衛聽說了歌利亞的挑戰，決定與那位勇士一戰。

他在心裡想：「主，我們的神保佑著我們。祂會保護我不被這個勇士打敗。」

他撿起五顆平滑的大石子，放進他的袋子裡。然後他朝非利士人的營地走去。

歌利亞看見大衛走來，他氣怒了。「這小夥子是何許人，以色列人竟派他來跟我交手？他們以為這是可笑的遊戲嗎？我會殺了你，把你的頭插在我的矛上，展示給他們看！」

p. 74–75 歌利亞吶喊著衝向大衛。大衛佇立不動,並從袋子裡取出一顆石子。他把石子裝到投石器上,然後開始將投石器甩到頭頂上方揮動著。

突然,他讓石子從投石器中飛了出去,石子正中歌利亞的額心,歌利亞仆倒在地。

大衛向他衝過去,拔出歌利亞的劍。大衛割下歌利亞的首級,高舉展示給非利士人看。

非利士人看見他們的英雄首級在大衛的手中,他們嚇壞了,轉身逃走。許久之後,大衛成為以色列之王。

［第五章］ 所羅門王

p. 78 大衛死後,他的兒子所羅門登基為王。一天,兩名婦人來到所羅門御前。她們想要他解決她們的爭執。其中一名婦人抱著一個嬰兒。

第一個婦人說:「所羅門王,請聽我們的事。這個婦人和我都生了寶寶。一天晚上,這個婦人的寶寶死了。她把她的死嬰抱到我的房間。趁我睡著時,她抱走了我的寶寶!」

「騙子!」另一個婦人喊道:「妳說的不是實情!」

p. 80 所羅門王喝令：
「拿劍把嬰兒砍成兩半。
然後把兩半各分給兩
女。這樣一來，她們兩
個都會滿意了。」

「不要！」第一個
婦人喊道：「寶寶給她
吧。我（雖然）失去他，
而他活著，這樣總比較
好。」

第二個婦人嚷道：「這個決定好。」

所羅門王聽到（雙方）這番話，他對第一個婦人說：「妳一
定是這個寶寶的親生母親。沒有一個母親會容許她的孩子被殺
死。」

人們聽聞了這項裁決，他們知道他們的國王是睿智的好國王。

但以理與獅群

p. 82-83 但以理是一個從耶路撒冷
被擄走的以色列囚犯。波斯在戰爭
中打敗了以色列，波斯國王要許多
年輕的猶太人服侍他，但以理就是這批年輕人之一。

但以理長大後，波斯換了新的國王當政，他的名字是大流士。
大流士王真心喜歡但以理，但以理現在是個非常有智慧的好人，
於是大流士任命但以理擔任波斯最重要的官職。

波斯許多其他的官員都忌妒但以理，他們試圖想出某種法子，
讓大流士對但以理生氣，可是但以理是個非常誠實的人，他的敵
人在但以理身上找不到任何錯處。

p. 84-85 但是有一天，一名波斯官員想到了一個主意。所有官員都去晉見大流士。

他們告訴大流士，波斯國內非常混亂，「人民向許多不同的神祇求問許多不同的事，」他們說：「您應該制定一條新法。在未來的三十天內，任何人不准祈禱。」

「要是有人被發現在祈禱，那會如何？」大流士王問道。

「那麼他就要被扔進關著獅群的洞穴，」官員們回答。

大流士王簽署了新法。但以理聽到這條新法時，他很難過，卻不能中止作祈禱。他回到他的房間，向天主禱告。官員們瞧見了這個舉 ，便報告國王。大流士下令逮捕但以理。

p. 86-87 但以理被押到獅穴。國王說：「你的神會找到法子救你。我沒法子。」

接著守衛便將但以理送進獅穴。他們用一塊大岩石壓住穴口。大流士王難過得吃不下，喝不下，也睡不著。翌晨，他飛奔到獅穴。但以理站在那兒，毫髮無傷！大流士王驚訝極了。

但以理說：「我主派遣一位天使，來堵住群獅的嘴。」

大流士王這才知道，但以理的神的力量。

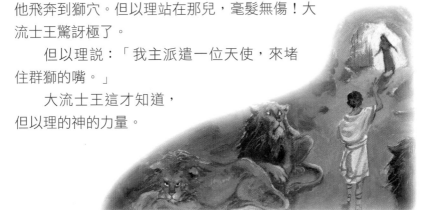

Answers

P. 26
A ① grass ② earth ③ snake

B ① sixth ② sixth ③ first ④ fourth ⑤ seventh

P. 27
C ① apple ② ribs ③ jealous ④ afraid ⑤ leave

D ① T ② F ③ F ④ T

P. 42
A tower, brick, rise up, clay, language

B ① forty / forty ② Two
③ one hundred and fifty

P. 43
C ① was caused ② took ③ grew ④ felt

D ① F ② T ③ F

E ③ → ② → ① → ④

P. 60
A ① You shall not commit murder.
② You shall have no gods but me.
③ Remember the Sabbath day, and keep it holy.
④ You shall not be jealous of your neighbor.

P. 61
B ① (c) ② (b)

C ② → ③ → ④ → ①

P. 76
A ① Samson ② Goliath ③ David
④ Delilah

B ① challenge ② warrior ③ pillars ④ sling

P. 77　C　**1** (c)　**2** (c)

　　　　D　**1** T　**2** F　**3** F　**4** T

P. 88　A　**1** judgment, wise, David's son

　　　　B　**1** have thrown　**2** has solved　**3** has made
　　　　　　4 has ordered

P. 89　C　**1** (b)　**2** (b)

　　　　D　**1** F　**2** T　**3** T　**4** F

P. 104　A　**Moses:**　**1** He was born in Egypt. God told him
　　　　　　　　　　　to save the Jews.
　　　　　　Adam:　**2** He was the first man.
　　　　　　David:　**3** He was a young shepherd.
　　　　　　　　　　　He killed a strong warrior.
　　　　　　Samson:　**4** He was the strongest king of Israel.
　　　　　　　　　　　He killed many Philistines.

　　　　B　**1** Samson lost his strength when Delilah tied him
　　　　　　　with new ropes. (F)
　　　　　　2 Noah brought two of every animal into his
　　　　　　　boat. (T)

　　　　C　**1** created　**2** let, go　**3** ordered

P. 105　D　**1** Why did people stop working on the tower of
　　　　　　　Babel? (b)
　　　　　　2 Who was thrown into the lions' cave for praying
　　　　　　　to God? (b)

　　　　E　**1** Cain killed Abel (b)
　　　　　　2 Solomon found the real mother (c)
　　　　　　3 Adam and Eve left the Garden of Eden (a)

Adaptors of *Bible Stories*

Brian J. Stuart

University of Utah (Mass Communication/Journalism)
Sookmyung Women's University, English Instructor

聖經故事【二版】
Bible Stories

作者 _ Brian J. Stuart

插圖 _ Ludmila Pipchenko

翻譯 _ 王啥

編輯 _ 多多

校對 _ 林晨禾

封面設計 _ 林書玉

排版 _ 葳豐企業有限公司

播音員 _ Sean Logan, Nancy Kim

製程管理 _ 洪巧玲

發行人 _ 周均亮

出版者 _ 寂天文化事業股份有限公司

電話 _ +886-2-2365-9739

傳真 _ +886-2-2365-9835

網址 _ www.icosmos.com.tw

讀者服務 _ onlineservice@icosmos.com.tw

出版日期 _ 2019年5月 二版一刷（250201）

郵撥帳號 _ 1998620-0 寂天文化事業股份有限公司

國家圖書館出版品預行編目資料

聖經故事【二版】/ Brian J. Stuart 著；—
二版. —[臺北市]：寂天文化，2019.5 面；公
分. 中英對照

ISBN 978-986-318-804-9 (25K平裝附CD)

　　1. 英語　　2. 讀本

805.18　　　　　　　　　　108006668